My Secret Unicorn

Rising Star

Lauren gasped as a wave of water rushed
down the creek towards them. It swept over
the bridge, submerging it completely . . .
'How are we going to get back?'
Grace exclaimed in alarm. Lauren looked
round but there was no other way off the
island. Grace and Currant were trapped.

My Secret Unicorn

Rising Star

Linda Chapman

Illustrated by Ann Kronheimer

PUFFIN

PUFFIN BOOKS

UK | USA | Canada | Ireland | Australia
India | New Zealand | South Africa

Puffin Books is part of the Penguin Random House group of companies
whose addresses can be found at global.penguinrandomhouse.com.

www.penguin.co.uk   www.puffin.co.uk   www.ladybird.co.uk

First published 2006
This edition published 2018

004

Written by Linda Chapman
Text copyright © Working Partners Ltd, 2006
Illustrations copyright © Ann Kronheimer, 2006
Created by Working Partners Ltd, London W6 0QT

The moral right of the author and illustrator has been asserted

Typeset in 14.25/21.5 pt Bembo
Printed in Great Britain by Clays Ltd, Elcograf S.p.A.

A CIP catalogue record for this book is available from the British Library

ISBN: 978-0-241-36309-6

All correspondence to:
Puffin Books
Penguin Random House Children's
80 Strand, London WC2R 0RL

*To Victoria Holmes – the undisputed Queen
of Good Ideas – for all the listening,
and the discussing, and for stopping me from
throwing my computer down the stairs!*

CHAPTER

One

Lauren Foster stood with her
unicorn, Twilight, in the woods
behind Orchard Stables. The sun had set
behind the Blue Ridge Mountains and
the sky was beginning to get dark. In a
nearby field, four ponies were grazing
peacefully. A fifth pony – who had a coat
the colour of dark-grey shadows and a
fluffy, sticking-up mane – was trotting

around them. Lauren watched him carefully. Currant belonged to her friend, Grace Wakefield, who lived at Orchard Stables. Lauren and Twilight had come here tonight for a very special reason!

Currant whinnied hopefully, and the other ponies looked up. Currant snorted and pawed the ground, but his friends just lowered their heads and carried on grazing. Lauren felt sorry for Currant. It was clear he wanted to play.

But she hadn't come here to watch Currant play. Lauren and Twilight had first seen him nearly a year ago, when he was a tiny foal. Ever since, they had suspected he might be a secret unicorn!

'Will we really find out if Currant is

a unicorn tonight?' Lauren whispered to Twilight.

Twilight nodded, his silver horn glinting in the starlight. 'Yes.'

Twilight's mouth didn't move, but Lauren could hear his voice clearly in her head. Most of the time, Twilight looked just like any other slightly scruffy, grey pony, but he had a very special secret. Whenever Lauren said the words of the Turning Spell, he transformed into a unicorn. Lauren had learnt there were other unicorns disguised as ponies all over the world. She really hoped Currant was one too!

'If Currant *is* a unicorn, a Unicorn Elder will visit him tonight,' Twilight went on. 'Unicorns who are born on Earth are always visited by an Elder on the night of their first birthday. The Elder tells them that they are not really a pony but a unicorn in disguise.'

The Unicorn Elders were the guardians of Arcadia, a magical land where most of the unicorns lived. The Elders watched over the Earth through a seeing stone, keeping an eye on all the unicorns that lived on Earth. Each secret unicorn had to try and find a human who was brave and good-hearted and who believed in magic enough to say the Turning Spell. The unicorn and their human friend would then try to help people and do good deeds.

'Will the Elder turn Currant into a unicorn tonight?' Lauren asked.

Twilight shook his head. 'No. Currant will have to wait until he finds his own special friend to say the Turning Spell before he can transform for the first time.'

As Twilight spoke his horn started to glow. It was a sign that his magic was at work. 'There's someone coming,' he said, listening with his super-sensitive unicorn hearing. 'I can hear footsteps.'

He and Lauren backed further into the shadows of the trees.

'It's Grace,' Lauren whispered as a tall girl with blonde hair came hurrying down the path towards the field.

Grace leant against the gate. 'Currant!' she called.

Seeing his owner, Currant trotted over, whinnying in delight.

'Hi, boy,' said Grace. She took a carrot from her pocket and held it out to him. 'I just wanted to see you before I go to bed. I can't believe it's your first birthday already! Only two more years and I'll be able to start riding you. We'll have so much fun together.'

Currant nuzzled her face.

'I love you,' Grace said softly. 'Goodnight.'

She kissed him. Currant nickered a goodbye as she walked away.

Grace turned and waved. 'Happy birthday, boy!'

Lauren watched her go. It would be

great if Currant *was* a unicorn and Grace had the chance to be his Unicorn Friend! Then the two of them could do all sorts of unicorn things together. There were only two other people who knew about Twilight's secret — Lauren's friend Michael, who lived in the city and who owned a unicorn called Moonshine, and Mrs Fontana, the old lady who ran the local bookstore. Mrs Fontana used to have a unicorn. She had told Lauren that unicorns really existed and given her a book about unicorns that contained the words of the Turning Spell.

'Oh, I hope Currant *is* a unicorn,' Lauren said, resting her head against Twilight's warm neck.

Twilight snorted in agreement.

The night darkened around them.
After a bit, Lauren's legs started to ache
from standing up, and she sat down on a
tree stump. She wondered how long
they would have to wait. Twilight rested
his chin on her shoulder and together
they watched as the ponies, even
Currant, settled down for the night.

Lauren had just started to yawn when
she felt Twilight's head shoot up.

'Lauren – look!' he exclaimed.

Lauren stared upward. A white shape
was cantering through the dark sky. 'It's
a Unicorn Elder!' Lauren said as a
magnificent unicorn swooped down
towards the field.

Four of the ponies snorted in surprise and trotted nervously away as the unicorn cantered to the ground. But Currant stayed exactly where he was, watching the unicorn with huge eyes.

The unicorn landed with a majestic toss of its head. Arching its sleek neck, it stepped towards Currant, its silver mane and tail rippling in the breeze.

'It's Sidra,' Twilight whispered. Sidra was the Elder who had visited Twilight before.

Stretching out her neck, Sidra whickered to Currant.

Lauren watched expectantly as Currant walked over to the unicorn. She felt so proud of him!

The foal and the Elder met in the

centre of the field. Sidra touched noses
with Currant and blew gently on to his
muzzle.

Currant tossed his head excitedly.

'He *is* a unicorn,' Twilight whispered
to Lauren. 'Sidra's just told him!'

Currant spun round. He cantered
away and stopped with a loud whinny as
if to say, *Look at me!* When the other
ponies stared, he reared up and struck
out at the air with his small hooves.

Sidra's dark eyes glowed with
amusement. Lifting her head, she tossed
back her flowing mane. Currant copied
her, although it didn't look as impressive
because his black-and-white mane was
short and stuck up in tufts.

Sidra cantered across the field and swept effortlessly into the air. Currant galloped along the grass beneath her, only stopping when he reached the fence. He pawed the grass impatiently as if he wished he could fly too.

Sidra swooped back over the paddock before vanishing into the starry sky.

Lauren hugged Twilight. Currant was a unicorn! 'I hope Grace is going to be Currant's Unicorn Friend!' she exclaimed.

'Me too. I wish we could just tell her to say the Turning Spell,' Twilight said.

'We can't,' Lauren reminded him. 'Unicorn Friends have to believe in magic enough to try the Turning Spell for themselves. If we told Grace that Currant was a unicorn, the magic wouldn't work.'

'I know,' replied Twilight. 'But we could help her a bit, couldn't we? We're allowed to tell her about unicorns even if we can't say that Currant is one.'

Lauren nodded. When she'd first bought Twilight at a pony sale, Mrs Fontana had given Lauren a book that told her everything about unicorns. 'We'll do everything we can to help her,' Lauren promised. 'Come on. It's time to go home.'

She climbed on to Twilight's back and he cantered into the air. As he rose higher, the wind blew through Lauren's long fair hair. 'Go as fast as you can, Twilight!' she cried.

Twilight surged forward until the stars blurred around them. Wrapping her hands in his long mane, Lauren laughed in delight. Having a unicorn was the best thing in the world!

CHAPTER
TWO

When Lauren woke up the next
morning, she felt a strange
feeling of excitement fizzing through
her. She lay in bed for a moment trying
to figure out why. It was the first day of
the holidays but that wasn't the only
reason she felt so excited. *Of course*, she
remembered suddenly. 'Currant's a
unicorn and we're going to try to help

Grace become his Unicorn Friend!' she whispered to herself.

Jumping out of bed in delight, Lauren threw open her curtains. She could see Twilight's paddock from her window. He was waiting by the gate for her. The sky was grey and a light drizzle was falling, but even the rain couldn't dampen Lauren's happiness. Currant was a unicorn! Pulling on her clothes, she ran downstairs.

Her mum was getting breakfast ready in the kitchen. 'You look like you're in a good mood,' she said as she got the plates out.

'I am!' Lauren grinned as Buddy, her brother Max's Bernese mountain dog, came bounding over to greet her. He wriggled against her legs, almost knocking her over. He then plonked himself down on her feet – his favourite way of greeting family and friends. 'Buddy, you weigh a ton!' Lauren groaned. Buddy thumped his tail on the floor and looked up at her lovingly. Bending down, Lauren gave him a hug. Although he was Max's dog, she loved him almost as much as she loved Twilight.

'So what are your plans for today?' Mrs
Foster asked and then she smiled. 'No. Let
me guess. They involve you spending the
whole day with Twilight – right?'

'Close,' Lauren said, leaving Buddy and
helping her mum set the table. 'Mel and
Jess are coming over and we're going to
go to Orchard Stables for a pony party,
remember? I told you about it.'

Mrs Wakefield, Grace's mum, had
invited Lauren and her two best friends,
Mel Cassidy and Jessica Parker, to ride
over to Orchard Stables that day. She was
holding a special party to mark the fifth
anniversary of the Wakefields buying
Orchard Stables – and to celebrate
Currant's birthday too!

'Oh yes,' her mum said. 'I bet Currant will enjoy being the centre of attention.'

Lauren nodded. Currant loved it when people made a fuss of him.

'He's such a sweet foal,' Mrs Foster commented.

Lauren grinned. If only her mum knew the truth! Hugging her secret to herself, she quickly ate breakfast, took an apple from the fruit bowl as a special treat for Twilight and ran down to the stables. Twilight whinnied eagerly when he saw her.

'Oh, Twilight,' Lauren said, climbing the gate. 'Isn't it wonderful about Currant?' He nodded and crunched up the apple she offered to him. 'I can't wait to see him today,' Lauren went on.

Twilight snorted in agreement, spraying bits of apple all over her.

'Thanks, boy,' Lauren said with a grin. She wiped down her jodhpurs and set about feeding and grooming him.

Mel and Jessica arrived just before noon. Lauren was tacking up Twilight when she heard the clatter of hooves. Looking round, she saw Mel on her dapple-grey pony, Shadow, and Jessica on her young, lively palomino, Sandy. They were riding down the track to meet her.

'Hi, Lauren!' Mel called. 'Are you ready to go? The party starts soon.'

'I'm ready,' Lauren said, pulling on her hard hat.

She mounted and they all rode down the track together. Orchard Stables bordered on to the back of Granger's Farm, and Lauren's dad let them ride through the farm as long as they stayed at the edges of the fields.

The first two fields had cows in and the girls rode at a steady walk and trot, but the next field was empty.

'Race you to the gate!' Lauren cried.

Twilight leapt forward, quickly followed by Sandy and Shadow. They reached the gate in a dead heat. Laughing and breathless, the girls patted their mud-spattered ponies and let them walk across the last field to cool down before they reached Orchard Stables.

'Look!' Jessica exclaimed as they rode up the drive.

Lots of people were gathered in the outdoor schooling ring, some on ponies, others on foot. Music was playing and streamers had been tied to the fence.

Two tables with bright-red tablecloths had been set up at the end of the ring. One was piled high with buckets of

apples and carrots, and the other was
laden with plates of sandwiches, iced
horse-shaped biscuits and an enormous
cake in the shape of a horseshoe.

Near the table, Lauren spotted Jo-Ann,
Grace's best friend. She was holding
Currant's mum, a pretty dapple-grey
mare called Apple. Lauren looked
around, but she couldn't see Currant.

'Hey, there's Grace!' Mel said, pointing
to the table.

Grace was putting a pile of plates
beside the cake. When she looked up,
she noticed the girls and came over. 'Hi!'

'The food looks great!' said Lauren.
'Where's Currant?'

'Mum thought I should leave him in

his stable until everything was ready,' Grace explained. 'He seems really excited today. I'm sure he knows it's his birthday party. He's been whinnying all morning!'

Lauren grinned. She knew *exactly* why Currant was so excited – and it wasn't just because of the party!

Mrs Wakefield, a tall woman with blonde hair, walked over. 'Hi, girls,' she said. 'Grace, do you want to go and get Currant now?'

Grace nodded and set off.

Mrs Wakefield went over to a table and picked up a megaphone. 'Welcome, everyone! As you know, we're celebrating five years at Orchard Stables, as well as Currant's first birthday.' She looked towards the stables. 'Here comes the guest of honour!'

Grace led Currant into the ring. His dark-grey coat gleamed. His tail, black at the top but turning to white at the bottom, had been washed and all the tangles had been combed out; his small, black hooves gleamed with hoof-oil.

He snorted loudly when he reached the gate and saw everyone waiting for him. Grace laid her hand on his neck and murmured a few words to reassure him. But Currant didn't look as if he needed soothing. With a toss of his head, he cantered forward, dragging Grace over to the tables.

'Steady, boy!' she gasped.

Currant skittered to a halt and grabbed a carrot from the plate, peeping out from under his forelock as he crunched it up. He looked very pleased with himself.

Everyone laughed.

'Happy birthday, Currant,' Mrs Wakefield said, going over and patting the foal.

'You're the most handsome foal in the world!' Grace told him.

'Certainly the cheekiest!' Mrs Wakefield remarked. 'OK, everyone! Help yourselves to some food.'

As people milled around the tables, Grace led Currant over to where Lauren, Mel and Jessica were standing with their ponies.

'Happy birthday, Currant,' Mel said, holding Shadow's reins in one hand and reaching out to pat Currant with the other.

Grace grinned. 'I think he likes birthday parties, don't you, boy?'

Currant nodded his head up and down.

Mel laughed. 'Look, he's saying yes!'

Grace seemed a bit embarrassed. 'This is going to sound really weird, but sometimes it seems like he understands everything I say.' Her cheeks went red. 'I know it's crazy!'

Lauren felt Twilight nudge her in the back. She hid a smile. If only the others knew!

'He's such a show-off,' Jessica teased, as Currant stamped the ground and whinnied.

'He is, but I love him to bits!' Grace said.

It was exactly how Lauren felt about Twilight. She was more convinced than ever that Grace would be a perfect Unicorn Friend.

Lauren watched Grace hugging Currant. She and Twilight had to find a way to help Grace discover her pony's secret!

After the party had finished, Lauren, Mel and Jessica rode back to Granger's Farm. As the ponies walked along the track to

Twilight's paddock they passed a flat
stretch of concrete. Lauren's dad had
made it into a mini skateboarding area
with ramps, steps, quarter pipes and rails
for Lauren's seven-year-old brother, Max,
to play on.

He was skateboarding there now with
his best friends – Stephen and Leo
Vance, who lived on the other side of
the woods. Buddy and Buggy, Stephen
and Leo's young flat-coated retriever,
were bounding around the skateboards,
getting in the way.

'Watch this!' Max cried when he saw
the girls riding past. He pushed his
skateboard along the ground, kicked
down on the back and jumped into the

air. The skateboard looked as if it was glued to his feet. He landed easily and skated on.

'Cool!' Lauren called.

Stephen, who was eleven and in Lauren's class at school, laughed. 'Way to go, Max! Now try this.'

He started showing Max another move. To Lauren, it looked almost exactly the same as the last trick, except Stephen's feet were in a different position. Max nodded and began trying it out.

'Hey, Stephen! Look at me!' called Leo, Stephen's nine-year-old brother. He skated towards a milk crate on its side and jumped over it.

'Yeah, that's good, Leo,' Stephen said,

glancing round briefly before turning back to Max. 'Hey, that's it!' he said as Max managed the new move that Stephen had just been teaching him. 'I couldn't do one of those till I was nine. You're a real skateboard ace, Max!'

Max beamed. 'Let's practise some kickflips now,' he said to Stephen.

'Sure,' said Stephen, picking up his board.

As Mel and Jessica rode on, Lauren glanced at Leo. He was standing a little way off, and she thought he looked a bit fed up. 'I thought your jump was really good, Leo,' she called to him.

'Thanks.' Leo sighed and skated off to practise by himself.

Neither Max nor Stephen seemed to notice how unhappy Leo was. Lauren wondered whether to say anything to them, but just then Mel called over to her to say that she and Jessica were heading home.

As Lauren trotted Twilight over to the others, her thoughts returned to Grace and Currant. How were she and Twilight going to help Grace become Currant's special unicorn friend?

I'll turn Twilight into a unicorn this afternoon, she decided. *We can talk about it then.*

★ ★

CHAPTER

Three

'Let's go to the secret clearing,' Lauren whispered to Twilight after lunch.

Twilight nodded and she quickly tacked him up. The secret clearing was a glade in the woods near Granger's Farm. Twilight pushed his way along a half-hidden, overgrown path until the trees opened out into a small circular

clearing. The rays of the spring sun
filtered down through the leaves. A
cloud of golden butterflies fluttered in
the air and star-shaped purple flowers
dotted the short, tufty grass. Looking
around, Lauren felt a rush of happiness.
The glade was one of her favourite
places in the whole world.

Jumping off Twilight, she said the
Turning Spell:

> *'Twilight Star, Twilight Star*
> *Twinkling high above so far.*
> *Shining light, shining bright,*
> *Will you grant my wish tonight?*
> *Let my little horse forlorn*
> *Be at last a unicorn!'*

In a bright purple flash Twilight
transformed into a unicorn.

Lauren hugged him. It was always
wonderful when he became a unicorn
again and they could talk properly. 'I
wish we could think of a way to help
Grace find out about Currant. But it
might seem weird if I start talking about
unicorns for no reason.'

Twilight thought for a moment.
'When we were trying to tell Michael
about Moonshine being a unicorn, you
lent him your unicorn book,
remember? After reading it, he tried
out the spell and Moonshine turned
into a unicorn. Why don't we do that
again?'

'What a good idea!' Lauren exclaimed. 'I'll invite Grace round tomorrow and leave the book where she can see it.'

'Perfect!' Twilight agreed happily.

As soon as Lauren got home, she rang Grace and asked her if she wanted to ride over the next day.

'Sure,' Grace replied. 'Apple could use some exercise. I'll come over around ten, if that's OK.'

Putting the phone down, Lauren only just managed to stop herself from jumping excitedly round the room. What would Grace say when she saw the unicorn book?

Lauren was up early the following morning. She tidied her bedroom and placed the unicorn book that Mrs Fontana had given her on her bed. It was a large purple book with very old pages. Its title was written in gold letters on the front: *The Life of a Unicorn*.

As Lauren went downstairs, she wondered how she was going to arrange for Grace to go up to her bedroom.

Usually when Grace rode over they just stayed outside with the ponies.

I'll have to think of an excuse for us both to go inside, she decided.

The sky was grey, and the clouds were so low that Lauren couldn't see the top of the mountain ridge behind the farm. As she and Twilight waited in his stable

for Grace to arrive, it started to rain.
When Grace rode up on Apple fifteen
minutes later, she and Apple were both
very wet.

'Yuck!' Grace said as she dismounted,
and heavy raindrops bounced off the
concrete by the stables. 'I'm soaked
through.'

Apple snorted and shook raindrops
from her mane.

Lauren saw her opportunity. This was
a perfect excuse to get Grace inside!
'Why don't we rub down Apple and put
her in a stable?' she suggested.
'Afterwards you can come into the
house and get dry too.'

Grace nodded and the two of them

set to work on the dapple-grey mare. Soon Apple was standing in a deep straw bed, wearing Twilight's sweat-sheet and munching on a haynet.

'Come on, let's go in,' Lauren said to Grace.

They hurried into the house.

Mrs Foster was in the kitchen. 'Oh, Grace!' she exclaimed. 'You're soaked! Come on, take off your coat. Let's get you dry clothes, a hot drink and something to eat.'

By the time Grace had put on a pair of Lauren's jodhpurs, dried her hair and eaten three cookies, she was looking happier. 'I can't believe it's raining *again*,' she said as she put down her mug of hot chocolate. 'It feels like it's been doing it non-stop for weeks, doesn't it? Dad says the creek in the woods near the bottom of our fields is going to overflow if the rain goes on like this.'

'Well, don't even think about going home until the rain stops,' Mrs Foster said, looking at the raindrops racing down the kitchen window. 'You can stay for lunch and if it's still raining later on, I'll give your mum a ring and see if she can come over with the horsebox.'

'Thanks, Mrs Foster,' said Grace.

'Now, I'd better get back to work,' said Mrs Foster. She was a children's author and often shut herself in her study for hours at a time when she was working on a book. 'Will you two be OK till lunchtime?'

'Fine,' Lauren said quickly. 'We can go hang out in my room, Grace.'

'OK,' Grace replied.

Lauren led the way up the stairs, her heart beating fast.

'I like your room,' Grace said as Lauren opened the door. She walked in and went to the little window seat. 'Cool. You can see Twilight's field from here.'

'Yes, if I sit up in bed I can watch him graze,' Lauren said. She sat on her bed and smoothed out the duvet cover, trying to draw Grace's attention to the book.

But Grace was looking at the pony posters on Lauren's wardrobe door. She

pointed to a picture of a black stallion.
'I've got that poster too!' She turned to
smile at Lauren. As she did so, her eyes
fell on the large purple book. 'What's
that book?' she asked curiously.

Lauren swallowed. 'Oh, just something
I was given.'

Grace picked it up. 'It's about
unicorns!' she exclaimed. 'I love
unicorns!'

'You do?' Lauren breathed.

'Oh yes,' enthused Grace. 'I wish they
were real.'

'But they are! I mean, well . . . er . . .
this book says they are,' Lauren said,
hastily correcting herself as Grace looked
at her in surprise. 'Have a look,' Lauren

said hurriedly as Grace began to flick through the pages.

Grace paused when she came to a picture of a small dark-grey pony – a drawing of a unicorn when it was in its pony form. Lauren knew it was the page that explained how to turn a unicorn into its magical shape.

'That looks like –' Grace started to say but then she broke off, looking embarrassed. 'It doesn't matter,' she said hastily. She sat down on the bed, holding the book open on her lap.

Hardly daring to breathe, Lauren watched Grace begin to read. Had she realized the grey pony in the picture looked a bit like Currant?

Grace turned a page and frowned thoughtfully as she saw a picture of a moonflower. 'You know, I've seen some of these flowers before,' she said.

'You have?' Lauren said in surprise.

'Yes, there's a clearing in the woods. I've been there a few times and there are flowers just like this growing in the grass.' Grace read on quickly. 'This book says they're called moonflowers and you need them to turn a unicorn into its magical shape for the first time . . .' Her voice trailed off. She looked up at Lauren. 'Oh wow,' she said softly. 'Just imagine if all this was true . . .'

Lauren saw a faraway, excited look in

Grace's eyes. 'You can borrow the book if you like,' she suggested eagerly.

'Really?' Grace said.

Lauren nodded.

'Thanks, Lauren!' Grace closed the book and hugged it to her. 'Thank you so much!'

By lunchtime the rain had slowed to a drizzle and after they had finished eating some weak rays of sunlight were peeping through the clouds.

Grace hadn't said much at lunch. But Lauren hadn't minded at all. She could guess what was on Grace's mind.

'I think I might head home now,' Grace said while they cleared their dishes away. 'Just in case it starts raining again.'

'Sure,' Lauren said.

'See you soon,' Grace called as she set off with the unicorn book safely in her backpack. 'Thanks for lending me the book, Lauren!'

As she rode off, Lauren noticed that Grace wasn't heading towards the fields. Instead, she had turned down the track into the woods. It was possible to get back to Orchard Stables through the woods, but it took a lot longer. Lauren crossed her fingers. Was Grace going home that way so she could stop at the moonflower clearing?

Lauren tacked up Twilight and waited

ten minutes before riding him into the woods too. As they came round a bend, she saw Apple and Grace coming out from the overgrown track that led away from the secret glade.

Lauren grinned to herself. Had Grace just picked a moonflower? If she had, surely that meant she was going to try out the spell!

She rode Twilight into the clearing. As soon as they were standing on the short grass, Lauren gabbled out the spell.

'I think our plan's worked!' she told Twilight when he had turned into a unicorn. 'Do you think Grace might be planning to turn Currant into a unicorn tonight? The book will tell her that the

first time she changes him into a
unicorn she has to say the spell when
the Twilight Star is shining.'

Twilight pawed the ground. 'Currant
is going to be so pleased that he's found
a Unicorn Friend already. Shall we use
my seeing magic to watch them later?'

'Great idea!' Excitement fizzed
through Lauren. She couldn't wait to see
whether Grace was going to say the
spell that night!

CHAPTER

Four

A s Lauren rode Twilight back towards
his field, she saw Max skateboarding
again with Stephen and Leo.

'That's it, Max!' Stephen called
encouragingly as Max tried a move that
involved him skating along, jumping and
spinning in the air. 'You just need to keep
your balance over the middle of the board
more, and try to keep going afterwards.'

Lauren looked round for Leo. He was zooming towards a set of two steps that Mr Foster had made. 'Hey, you guys, watch this!' he called. Pushing off at the top of the steps, he flew through the air on his board and landed safely. It looked like a very difficult jump and a broad grin spread across Leo's face. 'Did you see that downstairs ollie I just did?' he cried.

But Stephen was too busy watching Max. 'That's it!' he was saying. 'Now go faster, Max —'

'You didn't watch!' Leo protested.

Stephen waved a hand vaguely at him. 'I'll watch later, Leo,' he said, not taking his eyes off Max. 'Max has almost got this. Cool!' he gushed as Max tried the

spin again. 'That's loads better. Now try
it a bit faster . . .'

Leo skated over to the side of the
skateboard area. Jumping off his board,
he folded his arms. He looked very
cross.

Lauren felt sorry for him. *It must be
hard for him*, she thought. He and
Stephen had always skated together, but
now Stephen seemed so keen to help
Max learn new tricks that he wasn't
taking much notice of his brother.

'Hi, Leo,' Lauren said, riding over.

'Hi,' Leo muttered.

'Are you going to skate some more
with Max and Stephen?' she asked.

Leo shook his head. 'I don't want to

do any more skating today.' He kicked
the ground unhappily.

Twilight nudged him gently with his
nose.

'Hi, boy,' Leo muttered, stroking
Twilight's neck. He and Stephen both
loved animals.

Lauren wished she could cheer Leo
up. 'I'm going to untack Twilight and
groom him,' she said. 'You can come and
help me if you want.'

Leo shrugged. 'OK.' He followed
Twilight and Lauren down the path.
When they reached Twilight's stable,
Lauren untacked him and fetched the
grooming kit.

'Have you ever groomed a pony
before?' she asked.

Leo shook his head. 'You've got loads
of brushes,' he commented, peering into
the grooming kit. 'Why do you need so
many?'

'Because they're all for different
things,' Lauren said. She handed him a
soft body brush. 'Twilight loves being
brushed with this. Do you want to try?'

Leo began to brush Twilight's neck.
Twilight sighed happily. Leo's strokes

grew more confident and his face started to relax. 'He does like it, doesn't he?' he agreed.

Lauren nodded as she started to clean out Twilight's hooves.

After grooming Twilight's neck, Leo brushed Twilight's mane. Twilight turned his head and rested his muzzle on the boy's shoulder. Leo smiled. 'I like grooming Twilight.'

Lauren smiled back, glad to see he was looking happier. 'He likes it too.'

Just then there was the sound of voices. Max and Stephen were coming down the path with their skateboards.

'Leo!' Stephen called to his brother. 'Why did you stop skating?'

The smile faded from Leo's face. He shrugged. 'Just did.'

'Well, we should go home now,' Stephen said, not seeming to notice his brother's unhappy expression. 'Mum told us to be back by four-thirty. See you tomorrow, Max.'

Max nodded eagerly. 'Can we practise doing one-hundred-and-eighties again?'

'Of course.' Stephen grinned at him. 'You're going to be the best skateboarder in your class when we go back to school.'

Max looked delighted.

Leo picked up his skateboard. 'Come on,' he said grumpily. 'Let's go.'

Looking surprised at his brother's

tone, Stephen said, 'OK. Well, see you, Max. Bye, Lauren!'

'Bye,' Lauren replied. She watched Leo stomp away up the lane. It looked as though he was feeling very left out, but Stephen still hadn't noticed.

'Can I help you put Twilight in his field?' Max asked, interrupting her thoughts. He loved Twilight, although he didn't ride him regularly.

Lauren smiled at him. 'Of course. You can ride him bareback while I lead him if you like. Come on!'

Supper was macaroni cheese and salad. Afterwards, Lauren helped clear the dishes. The sun was beginning to sink in the sky. Lauren knew that the Twilight Star appeared each night just as the sun set. She needed to turn Twilight into a unicorn before then so they could use his magic to watch Grace.

Her dad was putting on his coat. 'I'm going to the Cassidys' to take a look at their video camera before I buy one tomorrow. What are you guys up to this evening?'

'I have to help Max with his project for school and then I've got lots of work to do,' Mrs Foster said, running a hand through her hair. 'I just can't seem to get the chapter I'm writing to work out. Will you be OK amusing yourself, Lauren? You can put a DVD on if you like.'

'I might watch one later,' she said. 'Can I go and see Twilight first?'

'Again? You've been with him all day, Lauren!' Mrs Foster said.

'You'll be asking if you can move your bed into his field next!' Lauren's dad teased.

Lauren grinned. 'Well, actually . . .'

'No!' Mrs Foster said firmly, but she was smiling. 'Of course you can go and see him now. Come in when it gets dark.'

'I will,' Lauren promised. She pulled on her trainers and, when her dad had driven off and her mum had gone upstairs with Max, she hurried to see Twilight.

'We're safe,' she told him as she

climbed over the gate. 'Dad's gone out and Mum's busy.'

They hurried to the far end of the field and Lauren said the spell. In an instant Twilight became a unicorn again.

'We can use one of these stones to see Grace,' he said, touching his horn to a rock near the trees. It looked almost black in the darkness but Lauren knew that in the daylight it gleamed a pinky-grey colour because it was made of rose quartz. Twilight could use his powers to turn it into a magic mirror that showed what was happening anywhere in the world.

Lauren slipped off his back and he touched his horn to the stone.

'Orchard Stables. Grace,' he murmured.

Purple mist swirled over the rose quartz. After a few seconds, the mist cleared and the surface of the stone began to shimmer. Looking into it, Lauren saw a picture of the fields at Orchard Stables. It was a bit like watching television.

'There's Currant's field,' she said, seeing a field with five ponies in it. Currant was standing by the gate. Lauren frowned. 'But where's Grace?'

'There!' Twilight said, pointing with his horn to the path that led to the field. Grace was walking down the path towards Currant.

'She's got the book!' Lauren breathed.

The foal whinnied. Grace stroked his mane and said something to him.

Lauren leant closer. The nearer you were to a seeing stone the better you could hear what people were saying. The faint buzz of a voice became clearer.

'Oh, Currant, I really hope this works,' Lauren heard Grace say.

'She's going to try out the spell!' Lauren said in delight to Twilight.

'Yes, it's –' Twilight broke off and frowned – 'Where's she going?'

Grace had turned away from the gate and was heading to the next field, where Apple was grazing.

'What's she doing?' Lauren wondered out loud as Grace climbed over the gate

and walked towards the grey mare.
Currant stood on the other side of the
fence, watching.

Looking excited but nervous, Grace
patted Apple and pulled a hair out of
her mane. Next Grace opened the
unicorn book at the page where the
spell was written. She glanced up at the

sky, where the Twilight Star shone like a chip of polished glass. Holding a moonflower from the secret clearing, she began to crumble the petals as she read the words out loud:

'Twilight Star, Twilight Star,
Twinkling high above so far . . .'

Suddenly Lauren realized what was happening. 'Oh, no! Grace must think Apple is a unicorn!'

Twilight snorted in dismay. 'Apple?'

Grace continued with the spell. As she reached the last lines she threw the remaining petals on the ground.

'Let my little horse forlorn
Be at last a unicorn!'

There was a bright purple flash.

Grace gasped and rubbed her eyes.

But when she lowered her hands again, Apple was still standing in front of her, looking exactly the same. Grace's face fell. 'Oh,' she whispered sadly. 'I thought –'

She was interrupted by a joyful whinny.

Grace swung round.

'Look!' Lauren whispered to Twilight.

Standing proudly on the other side of the fence where Currant had been was a little white unicorn!

CHAPTER
Five

'Currant!' Grace cried. 'You're a unicorn!'

'Oh, Twilight, isn't he cute!' Lauren murmured. Currant was a perfect snowy-white colour like Twilight, but he was a baby unicorn with long legs and a forelock, and a mane and tail that fluffed up instead of hanging in silken strands like Twilight's. Lauren noticed another

difference. 'His horn's golden!' she
exclaimed.

'Unicorns have different-coloured
horns,' Twilight explained. 'Some have
gold horns, some silver and some
bronze.' He sounded distracted — as if
something was bothering him. 'But I
don't understand. The spell shouldn't
have worked. Grace was holding a hair

from Apple's mane and she should have been holding a hair from Currant's.'

'That's true,' Lauren said. She thought back over what had happened. Grace had come to the field, stroked Currant, then gone over to Apple. 'I know!' Lauren exclaimed. 'I bet a hair from Currant's mane snagged on Grace's clothes before she went to see Apple.'

'Of course!' Twilight agreed. He peered into the seeing stone. 'Doesn't Grace look pleased?'

Lauren looked at the image in the quartz stone. Grace had scrambled over the fence and flung her arms around Currant's neck. Lauren leant forward to hear what Grace was saying, but then she hesitated. She remembered the time she had first turned Twilight into a unicorn. It had been one of the most special, most perfect moments of her life. It had also been one of the most private — just her and Twilight. How would she have felt if someone had been listening in?

She drew back from the stone. 'I think we've seen enough for tonight,' she said.

Lauren could tell that Twilight understood. He lifted his horn from the rock and the picture faded.

Lauren sighed happily. 'Isn't it brilliant that Grace is Currant's Unicorn Friend?' A thought struck her. 'He's very young, though. Will Grace be able to fly on his back?'

'Not yet,' Twilight replied. 'He won't be able to carry someone until he's three years old – just like a normal pony. But I expect she'll have lots of fun with him until then.'

Lauren hugged Twilight. 'You're right. I bet she will!'

Lauren dreamt about Grace and Currant that night. She imagined them all doing magic together and woke up grinning. It would be so cool to have a friend with a secret unicorn too. She wondered what Grace would say when she found out that Twilight was a unicorn like Currant!

As she was helping clear away the breakfast things the next morning, the phone rang. 'It's Grace, for you, Lauren,' said her dad, holding out the receiver.

'Hi, Lauren!' said Grace. She sounded breathless and excited. 'Is it OK if I ride Apple over and bring your book back? I don't think I need it any more!' She hastily corrected herself. 'I mean I . . . er . . . I've finished reading it. Can I come round in half an hour?'

'Sure,' said Lauren. 'See you then.' Putting the phone down, she raced outside as soon as she could to tell Twilight.

'Grace is coming over! Do you think she'll say anything about Currant?' Twilight whinnied excitedly.

Although Lauren couldn't understand exactly what he was saying, now that he was a pony again, she could tell he was just as keen as she was to hear what Grace had to say.

Half an hour later, Grace rode up on Apple. She was carrying the book under her arm. 'Here you go,' she said,

dismounting and handing the book to Lauren. Lauren had the feeling that she was trying as hard as she could to act normally. 'It's really . . .' Grace hesitated, '*interesting*.'

'It is, isn't it?' Lauren agreed innocently.

Grace's cheeks had gone red. 'Did you know it's –' She broke off. 'Oh, nothing,' she said, looking flustered. 'I'd better go.' She turned to mount Apple.

'It's OK, Grace,' Lauren said quickly. 'I know.'

Grace turned round very slowly to look at Lauren. 'You know?' she repeated in a whisper.

Lauren nodded. 'I know about unicorns.'

Grace stared at her. 'But . . . but how?'

Lauren glanced at Twilight, who was watching them over the fence.

Grace followed her gaze. 'Is Twilight a —'

'Ssh,' Lauren whispered.

They looked at each other.

'Currant is too,' Grace breathed. 'I tried the spell last night. It worked, Lauren. But Currant said I wasn't allowed to tell anyone.'

'Don't worry, you can tell other Unicorn Friends.' Lauren looked round and saw her dad coming down the path towards them. 'Look, it's not safe to talk now. Let's meet tonight. Twilight and I will fly to Currant's paddock. Wait for us there.'

Grace's eyes widened. 'You're going to *fly* there?'

'Of course,' Lauren said. 'Twilight and I go flying almost every night.'

'Wow!' gasped Grace.

Lauren glanced over her shoulder. Her dad was getting closer every second. 'We can talk more tonight. Eleven o'clock. In Currant's field.'

Grace nodded. 'We'll be there!'

Mr Foster walked up. 'You two look like you're plotting something. What's going on?' he asked curiously.

'Nothing,' Lauren replied.

'We're just planning when we'll next meet up,' Grace put in truthfully. 'Well, I'll see you, Lauren.'

'Yeah, see you,' Lauren replied, grinning at her.

As Grace rode off, Mr Foster smiled. 'It's great you've got so many friends to go riding with, Lauren.'

And now I've got someone to do magic with, too, Lauren thought in delight. She couldn't wait!

CHAPTER
Six

Just before eleven, Lauren turned
Twilight into a unicorn and they set
off for Orchard Stables. They swooped
across the fields and over the trees. Lauren
felt a rush of delight as the wind blew
against her cheeks and ruffled her hair.
There was nothing better than flying!

'There they are!' she cried, suddenly
spotting Grace and Currant waiting in

the shadows at the edge of his field. The other ponies were all dozing quietly near the gate.

As Twilight drew closer, he whinnied in greeting and the ponies by the gate jumped in surprise and put their heads up. Currant whinnied back, and Grace's mouth hung open in amazement as Twilight flew towards them. He landed smoothly on the grass beside them, his horn glinting in the starlight.

'I'm a unicorn, Twilight! I'm a unicorn!' Currant exclaimed.

'I can see!' Twilight laughed.

'Don't I look great?' Currant whinnied, shaking his mane proudly.

'I can understand what Currant's

saying!' Lauren said in surprise to Twilight.

'Unicorn Friends can understand all unicorns,' he explained. 'It's part of the unicorn magic.'

Lauren slid off Twilight's back and walked over to Grace, while Twilight touched noses with Currant. 'I'm so pleased you're a Unicorn Friend too,

Grace,' Lauren said. 'We'll be able to do all kinds of stuff together.'

'I've been telling myself all day that I've got a unicorn but it just doesn't seem real,' Grace replied, looking dazed. 'I keep thinking I must be about to wake up!'

Lauren grinned. She remembered feeling exactly the same when she'd first found out about Twilight being a unicorn.

Currant pushed his head between them. 'Hi, Lauren!'

Lauren laughed. 'Hi, Currant. Your horn's very glittery.'

Currant looked delighted at the compliment. 'It is, isn't it?'

'Twilight is such a beautiful unicorn,'

Grace said, glancing across to where
Twilight was standing.

'What about me, Grace?' Currant
demanded, pushing her impatiently with
his nose. 'Do I look beautiful too?'

Grace chuckled and turned her
attention to the foal. 'Of course you do.'

'Very beautiful,' Lauren told him,
although, to be truthful, Currant looked
more cute than beautiful. Twilight, on
the other hand, really did look stunning
in his unicorn form. For a moment she
saw him through Grace's eyes. His white
coat gleamed in the starlight, his neck
was arched and his tail swept the
ground. He looked very different from
how he looked normally.

'It was amazing to see you flying, Twilight,' Grace told him. 'You looked so graceful.'

'Thank you,' he said, sounding pleased.

'I bet *I'll* be really good at flying too,' Currant declared.

'Have you tried yet?' Lauren asked him.

Currant shook his head.

'Why don't you try now?' Grace suggested.

'Yes, go on,' Twilight encouraged the foal.

'OK.' Currant trotted forward and jumped into the air. 'I'm doing it!' he gasped as he cantered upward. His ears pricked forward. 'Whee! Look at me!'

He went faster and faster, but then his legs suddenly seemed to go in all directions at once.

'Are you OK?' Lauren called anxiously as he wobbled dangerously.

'Help! How do I turn round?' Currant cried, as he headed straight for a tree, his legs kicking and flailing.

Twilight leapt into the air and galloped up to him. Nudging the foal with his shoulder, he steered him away from the tree and back down towards the girls.

As he landed Currant stumbled to a halt, almost hitting his nose on the grass. Shaking his head, he looked up and tried to act as if he'd meant to land like that. 'Told you I could do it!' he said breezily.

Lauren and Grace's eyes met for a second.

'That was great, Currant,' Grace said carefully. 'But maybe . . .' She hesitated.

'Maybe you still need a bit more practice,' Lauren finished tactfully.

Currant seemed disappointed that they weren't more impressed. 'Oh.'

'You'll get better at flying soon,' Twilight promised. 'I was really wobbly at first too.'

'You're not wobbly at all now,' Grace said admiringly. 'Will you show me some flying, Twilight?'

'Sure!' Twilight answered. 'Come on, Lauren!'

Lauren scrambled on to his warm

back and they took off into the sky. As
the wind streamed past them, Twilight
swooped in a circle, jumped over two
treetops and turned a loop the loop
before flying back down to land just in
front of Grace.

'That was fantastic!' Grace gushed. 'I
wish I knew what flying felt like.'

Lauren opened her mouth to offer
Grace a go on Twilight, but then

stopped. *Twilight's mine*, she thought. *I don't want anyone else to fly on him*.

She felt awful for having such a mean thought. *Don't be so horrid*, she told herself. *You should share Twilight. Grace would love to fly on his back. Ask her if she wants to try*.

But the words just wouldn't come out of her mouth.

Twilight stirred beneath her. He began to step towards Grace but stumbled, almost falling on to his knees, even though there was nothing on the ground for him to trip over. He stood up again and pawed at the ground.

Lauren forced herself to speak. 'Ummm, Grace . . .' She licked her dry

lips. It was hard to get the words out –
as if something inside her was stopping
them.

Grace looked at her eagerly. 'Yes?'

Making a great effort, Lauren forced
out the words, 'You can have a –'

Before she could finish her sentence, a
wave of dizziness swept over her. She
caught her breath and grabbed Twilight's
mane.

'What's the matter, Lauren?' Grace
asked in alarm.

'I don't feel well,' Lauren said faintly.

Putting her arms round Twilight's
neck, she slid off his back, holding on
tight to his mane to stop herself from
crumpling to the ground. He turned and

nuzzled her anxiously. 'Are you OK, Lauren?'

Lauren blinked. 'I don't know. I just feel really dizzy.'

Letting go of him, she sank down till she was sitting on the ground. She covered her eyes with her hands. She felt as if she'd just got off a roundabout that had been spinning very fast.

Something touched her forehead. She opened her eyes. Twilight had bent down and was rubbing her head with his glowing horn.

She felt as if a curtain was being drawn back in her head. Her mind cleared and the dizziness vanished.

'Thanks, Twilight,' Lauren said shakily.

'I feel better.' She blinked. 'I . . . I don't know what happened.'

'Maybe you're coming down with something,' Grace said, looking worried. 'Do you think you should go home?'

'No. I feel OK now,' Lauren said, standing up.

'Did you help Lauren with magic, Twilight?' Grace asked.

Twilight nodded.

'Cool!' Grace breathed.

'Will I be able to do that one day?' Currant burst in.

Twilight snorted. 'Maybe.' His eyes flickered with amusement. 'Although you should probably concentrate on learning to fly first,' he said. 'Why don't you have

another go? You'll be better at it this
time. Come on, let's fly together.'

'I'll stay here,' Lauren said. She didn't
want to leave Grace on her own.

Twilight looked at her. 'Are you sure
you're OK, Lauren?'

'I'm fine,' Lauren promised.

The two unicorns soared into the sky,
but even with Twilight beside him
Currant still looked very wobbly. He
didn't seem to be able to stop or turn at
all and Twilight had to keep nudging
him in the right direction.

'Be careful!' Grace called as Currant
almost flew into a bush. 'Maybe you
should come down now.'

Twilight and Currant landed.

'Don't worry. You'll soon get the hang of it,' Twilight reassured Currant.

Lauren nodded. 'It'll just take a bit of practice.'

Currant looked up at them hopefully.

'Shall we all meet again tomorrow?' Grace asked.

'Definitely,' Lauren replied. 'See you then.'

She got back on to Twilight. As they took off, Lauren glanced at Grace and saw a wistful expression on her face. Lauren's stomach twisted in a guilty knot. She felt really mean that she hadn't offered Grace a ride on Twilight.

'Lauren, you're very quiet,' Twilight said.

'I just feel bad,' Lauren said, sighing.

'Grace wanted to know what flying was like. I should have offered her a go on you and I don't know why I didn't.' She blushed, thinking how selfish she'd been. 'I was going to,' she remembered, 'but then I felt dizzy and forgot about it. Now I feel awful.'

To her surprise, Twilight sighed too. 'I know,' he said. 'I could tell Grace wanted

to fly on me and I was going to offer, but when I tried to get the words out, my legs went all wobbly.'

Lauren frowned. 'Do you think something magical was happening?'

'I don't know,' Twilight replied. 'It's weird that we both felt like that, though —' He broke off. 'Lauren, look! It's Mrs Fontana!'

An old lady was walking through the woods with a black-and-white terrier bounding at her heels. Although it was very dark, Mrs Fontana wasn't carrying a torch. She strode along as if it was as light as day.

'Let's go and tell her about Currant!' Lauren cried.

Seven

'**M**rs Fontana!' Lauren called as Twilight swooped down through the trees.

Mrs Fontana's wrinkled face creased into a broad smile. 'Hello. I was wondering if I'd see you two tonight.'

Twilight landed and Walter the terrier trotted over to him. Standing up on his back legs, the little dog licked Twilight's nose.

'What are you doing in the woods so late?' Lauren asked the bookstore owner.

'Oh, just taking Walter for a walk,' Mrs Fontana said, pulling her mustard-yellow shawl closer round her shoulders. 'And keeping my eyes open for any . . .' she paused, '*interesting* things that might be happening.' Her bright blue eyes twinkled.

Lauren had a feeling that Mrs Fontana knew exactly what she and Twilight had been doing that evening. 'You know about Currant!' she exclaimed.

'And about Grace?' Twilight added.

Mrs Fontana nodded. 'Yes, my dears. I'm delighted for them. Grace often

comes into my shop and I'm sure she'll
make a wonderful Unicorn Friend.'

'But how do you know?' Lauren
asked in astonishment.

Mrs Fontana smiled mysteriously. 'I
have my ways.' She changed the subject
before they could ask any more
questions. 'Now, tell me what adventures
you two have had lately.'

'We've been helping Grace find out about Currant,' Lauren explained. 'And now she knows he's a unicorn, we're trying to teach Currant how to fly.'

Twilight nodded.

'Good,' Mrs Fontana said. 'But remember, he and Grace must find out about his other magic powers on their own.'

Lauren nodded. It was one of the rules — every unicorn and his Unicorn Friend had to find out the unicorn's magic powers for themselves. Mrs Fontana had told Lauren that it was a test to see how clever and brave the unicorn and his friend were.

Twilight pawed the ground, reminding

Lauren of what they had been talking about before they saw the old lady.

'Mrs Fontana, something odd happened tonight,' Lauren said. 'Grace was saying how much she wanted to fly. I knew we should offer her a chance to fly on Twilight, but it felt –' she searched for the words – 'wrong, somehow. I wanted to give her a ride but, at the same time, I didn't want to. When I tried to offer her a turn, I felt really dizzy and Twilight tripped over. I feel like I was so mean!'

'Don't worry,' Mrs Fontana said soothingly. 'You mustn't feel guilty. The bond between a unicorn and his human friend is very special indeed. It wouldn't be right to let another person fly on Twilight. Unicorn magic made you feel dizzy even when you went against your inner feelings and forced yourself to offer Grace a ride, Lauren. The same with you tripping up, Twilight.'

Lauren felt as if a heavy weight had slid off her shoulders. 'Phew. I just thought I was being selfish.'

'A unicorn isn't something you can share, Lauren.' Mrs Fontana said. 'It shows how good-hearted you are that you felt bad for Grace not being able to fly, but you mustn't feel like that. She has her own unicorn now. She's very, very lucky.'

A thought occurred to Lauren. 'But I've let two people on Twilight before,

Mrs Fontana: Jo-Ann when she hurt herself falling off Beauty, and Jessica when she had run away from home. I didn't feel weird then.'

'That's because they *needed* to fly on him,' Mrs Fontana explained. 'It's OK to let people on to Twilight's back if you're helping them. But not if it's just for fun.'

'I see,' Lauren said.

Twilight nuzzled Lauren's arm. 'It's a pity Currant's so young. Grace is going to have to wait for ages to find out what flying is like.'

'That's true,' Mrs Fontana agreed. 'On the other hand, you could say that she's lucky to have discovered his secret while he's still so young. She's going to have the joy of watching him grow up — very few Unicorn Friends do that. Even though Grace might not be able to ride Currant yet, I'm sure they'll have lots of fun together.'

Walter scampered on down the path and gave a yap. Mrs Fontana nodded at him. Just then, Lauren felt a raindrop on her cheek.

'Well, my dears,' Mrs Fontana said to Lauren and Twilight, 'I should be getting on my way before we get wet. See you again soon, and keep trying with Currant. He'll learn to fly very soon, I'm sure.'

'Bye!' Lauren called.

She waved until Mrs Fontana

disappeared into the shadows, and then got on to Twilight's back.

'I feel much better now,' he said.

'Me too,' Lauren agreed, wrapping her hands in his mane as he took off into the sky. 'Come on. Let's go home before the rain really starts!'

The following morning Lauren jumped out of bed at seven o'clock. It was one of the best things about Twilight's magic. She never felt tired when she'd been out with him, no matter how late they'd come home. She hurried downstairs. There was no one about. Pulling on her jacket, she went outside. It was raining again!

Twilight whinnied when he saw her.

Lauren buckled on his head-collar. 'Come on, boy,' she said. 'It's time for breakfast!'

When Twilight had eaten his breakfast, Lauren tied him to the metal ring in the wall of the stable and started to groom him. She wondered if she should phone Mel and Jess and see if they wanted to go for a ride. She glanced out of Twilight's door. The sky was grey, although it was raining less now. Maybe she should just go round to Mel's house. They could always clean their tack, or hang out in Mel's bedroom and read her pony magazines.

From outside the stable she heard a faint woof. Going to the door, she saw Max, Leo and Stephen walking past with their skateboards. Max was throwing a toy for Buddy. The dog raced after it, splashing through the puddles and barking excitedly.

Lauren watched them. They seemed to be chatting together quite happily. Lauren felt relieved. 'I hope Max and Stephen don't leave Leo out today,' she said to Twilight.

He snorted in agreement and Lauren carried on brushing his coat.

Half an hour later Twilight's coat was clean and smooth and his mane and tail fell in silken strands. Lauren finished off by putting oil on his hooves. 'You look beautiful!' she declared. She glanced down at her navy jodhpurs, which were covered in hair, hay and dust. 'Can't say the same about me!' she said with a grin. She went to the door. 'I'm going to go and clean up. Then I'll call Mel to see what she's doing today. See you later.'

Twilight snorted and turned back to his haynet. As Lauren shut the door, she heard Max, Stephen and Leo shouting in the distance.

She wandered down the path to see what they were doing. All three boys were standing by the upturned milk crate. Max was trying to jump it. He fell off a few times but Stephen kept encouraging him to try again.

Leo was looking bored.

'I'm going to do some more downstairs ollies,' he said. 'Are you coming, Stephen?'

'Not yet,' Stephen said. 'I'm helping Max. That's it!' he called. 'Try again! You've almost got it.'

'Come on, Stephen,' Leo pleaded. 'I bet I can do the four set over there,' he said, pointing to the set of four steps.

'That's way too hard for you,' Stephen replied.

'No it's not,' Leo argued.

'Don't be dumb,' Stephen told him. Just then Max managed to land without falling off for the first time. 'Good jump, Max!'

Leo glared at Stephen. 'I bet I *can* do a four set!'

But Stephen didn't hear.

Leo swung round and marched towards the big set of steps with his board under his arm. 'Look at me!' he called as he jumped on his board.

Stephen and Max turned round.

'Leo, don't!' Stephen yelled, looking alarmed.

Leo ignored him and skated faster and faster towards the top of the steps.

Lauren's heart jumped into her mouth. Surely he wasn't really going to try jumping down all those steps?

'Wait!' Stephen started to run towards his brother. But it was too late. Leo had taken off. His board launched into the air.

Lauren gasped. For a moment it looked like Leo was going to keep his balance but then, as the board slammed down, Leo's arms flailed and the board flipped over.

Leo hit the ground with a sickening crunch, in a tangle of arms, legs and skateboard.

CHAPTER

Eight

Lauren ran over to Leo as he sat up,
clutching his ankle. Stephen and
Max sprinted over to him too.

'Are you OK?' Stephen asked.

Leo bit his lip. His face was very pale.
'My ankle hurts!'

Stephen crouched down beside him
and touched Leo's ankle.

'Ouch!' Leo gasped. Lauren could tell

he was trying not to cry. 'It really hurts,' he said through gritted teeth.

'It might be broken,' Stephen said.

'I'll go and get Mum or Dad!' Lauren called, racing back towards the house.

Her dad was in the kitchen, frowning over the instructions of his new video camera. He looked up as Lauren hurtled through the door. 'What's the matter?'

'Quick, Dad!' Lauren panted. 'Leo's fallen off his skateboard!'

Mr Foster jumped to his feet. 'Where is he?'

'By the steps in the skateboard area,' Lauren answered. 'Come on!'

Fifteen minutes later, Leo was sitting on a chair in the kitchen with his leg raised up on another chair and an ice pack wrapped round his ankle.

Mr Foster had said that it didn't look like his ankle was broken, just badly sprained. 'It will hurt for at least a week,' he warned Leo. 'You're going to have to stay off that skateboard till it's better.'

'But it's the holidays!' Leo protested.

'Look, why don't the rest of you go back outside?' Mr Foster said. 'I'll call you when your mum gets here, Stephen. I'll stick the TV on for you, Leo — unless you know anything about video cameras?' He pushed the box towards Leo. 'I'm afraid I'm a technology dinosaur, and I can't figure out how to make it work.'

Leo looked interested. 'We've got this camera at home,' he said. 'It's really easy to use.'

Mr Foster raised his eyebrows. 'Can you tell me what I'm doing wrong, then?'

He sat down opposite Leo. Lauren and the others went outside.

'Poor Leo,' said Max.

'I know,' Stephen agreed.

Buddy ran up with his toy in his

mouth. He plonked it down on top of Max's feet.

'Fetch!' Max cried, picking up the toy and throwing it as hard as he could down the path. Buddy raced off excitedly and Max dashed after him.

Lauren looked at Stephen. She could tell he was still worried about his brother. 'Leo's ankle will be better soon,' she said.

Stephen nodded. 'It's lucky he didn't hurt himself more badly. I don't know why he tried coming down those steps. It was a crazy thing to do.'

Lauren had a pretty good idea why Leo had done it. 'Um, I think he did it to try and impress you,' she said awkwardly.

Stephen looked at her in surprise. 'What do you mean?'

Lauren swallowed. She and Stephen got on fine at school, but it wasn't as if they were close friends. 'Well, you've been helping Max loads,' she said. 'And I think Leo has been feeling a bit left out.'

'He doesn't need help,' Stephen said. 'He's really good at skateboarding.'

'Yes, but it must be hard for him to see you give Max so much attention,' Lauren pointed out.

Stephen nodded. 'I guess he has been acting a bit strange this week.' He thought for a moment. 'I'll try to include him from now on, but I don't know how we're going to do that if he can't skateboard.' He ran a hand through his hair. 'I'll talk to Max this afternoon and figure something out.'

'Good luck!' said Lauren.

Stephen gave her a quick smile. 'Thanks for telling me about Leo.'

Lauren smiled back. 'No problem. See you later.'

She ran to Twilight's stable. *I'm glad Stephen knows about Leo*, she thought happily as she unbolted the door. *Now I just hope we can help Currant with his flying!*

That afternoon, Grace rang. 'Are you still OK to meet tonight?' she said in a whisper to Lauren.

'Yes, of course,' Lauren replied.

'Do you think we should meet somewhere else than in the field?' Grace hissed. 'I'm worried Mum might come out and check on the ponies. What if she sees Currant and Twilight as unicorns?'

'We can't let that happen,' Lauren said in alarm. 'Is there anywhere else we could meet? Somewhere more secret?'

'There's an island in the middle of the creek near Currant's field,' Grace suggested. 'It's in the woods and it's really well hidden.'

'Brilliant,' Lauren said. 'Let's meet there.'

'OK,' Grace replied. 'See you at eleven again!'

★

Just before eleven, Lauren crept out of the house and turned Twilight into a unicorn. 'Do you know where the island near Currant's field is?' she asked as she climbed on to his back.

He nodded. 'Yes. I've seen it when we've been flying. Come on. Let's go!'

They flew across the fields and into the woods by Currant's field. 'There's the island,' Twilight said, nodding down to where the swollen creek was running swiftly through the trees.

Lauren saw a small patch of land in the middle of the water. It wasn't very big but it had trees on it and looked like the perfect secret meeting place for her and Grace and their unicorns. A low wooden footbridge stretched from either bank of the creek to the island.

Twilight whinnied and Lauren saw Grace leading Currant through the trees.

'Hi!' Lauren called.

Currant whinnied back in greeting and Grace waved.

As Twilight swooped down to land on the island, Grace led Currant on to the bridge. It was a bit rickety and the river was running fast beneath it, but Currant didn't hesitate and walked over it bravely, his hooves clopping on the wood.

'Hi, Twilight,' he said eagerly as he reached them. 'I'm going to be really good at flying today!'

Twilight nuzzled him. 'Yes, I bet you are.'

Currant looked pleased. 'Shall I have a try now?'

Twilight nodded and Currant immediately cantered into the air. He did seem a little less wobbly than the day before. 'Look at me!' he cried, gaining speed and shooting past Twilight.

'Don't go too fast,' Grace warned.

'Yes, slow down!' Twilight agreed. 'Remember, you're still learning!'

'I'm fine!' Currant declared. 'Hey, watch this, Grace!' He began to fly a loop the loop. But halfway through, he spun out of control. 'Whoah!' he exclaimed in alarm.

'Currant!' Grace cried as the foal nosedived into a clump of brambles.

Lauren and Grace raced over.

'Currant! Are you OK?' Grace asked anxiously.

Currant struggled to untangle himself from the bramble bush. The long thorny branches clung to his mane and tail, and wrapped round his hooves and legs. 'Ow!' he said, shaking his head. 'There are lots of thorns sticking into me!'

Lauren felt a rush of relief. Currant didn't seem badly hurt. 'Stay still,' she told him. 'Twilight can get you out.'

Twilight was already swooping towards them. Landing on the grass, he touched the brambles with his glowing silver horn. There was a puff of purple smoke, and the brambles started to untangle from Currant.

'Wow!' Grace breathed.

'It's one of Twilight's magic powers,' Lauren explained, feeling very proud of him.

'You are clever, Twilight,' Grace said admiringly.

The last of the brambles curled away from Currant and he struggled out of the bush. There were leaves and thorns caught in his coat, and his mane was tuftier than ever.

'Oh, Currant,' Grace said. 'You shouldn't have tried doing a loop the loop like that.'

Currant's head drooped. 'I thought I could do it.'

'You're too little,' Grace sighed. 'Look, maybe you should wait a bit before doing any more flying.'

Currant looked at her in dismay. 'You think I can't do it!'

'Well . . .' Grace hesitated. Lauren could tell that she didn't want to hurt Currant's feelings. 'Maybe you should just wait a little while before trying any more,' Grace continued. Currant's head sank. 'It's all right,' she told him quickly. 'You're still very young. You're not a proper grown-up unicorn like Twilight yet.'

Currant swallowed hard. 'You think

he's much better than me, don't you?' he
said softly.

'Oh, Currant —' Grace started to say.

Twilight nuzzled him. 'Come on,
Currant. Let's have one more go. Just
take it slowly this time.'

Currant hesitated and then gave a
small nod.

'Follow me,' Twilight said, flying into
the air.

Currant followed him but, after he
had risen about two metres, he started
to sink again.

'Come on,' Twilight called over his
shoulder.

'I can't go any higher!' Currant
exclaimed. His legs cantered frantically

but he kept dropping until he was
standing on the ground. 'I can't fly any
more!' he said, looking shocked.

'Of course you can,' Lauren assured him.

'I can't!' Currant wailed.

Grace put her arm round him. 'You're
probably just tired,' she said.

'Will you turn me back into a pony
now, Grace?' Currant asked in a very
small voice.

Grace stroked his tufty mane. 'OK.'

Lauren and Twilight said goodbye and, as Grace led Currant back over the bridge, Lauren mounted Twilight and they began to fly home.

'That was weird,' Lauren said. 'Why couldn't Currant fly?'

'I don't know,' Twilight admitted. 'I've never seen that happen before.'

Lauren frowned. 'Do you think Grace could be right? Was he just tired?'

'I can't see why he would be,' Twilight replied. 'Currant's usually got lots of energy.' He shook his head. 'It was like his magic wasn't working properly.'

Lauren felt very worried. 'I hope he'll be OK tomorrow.'

Twilight snorted. 'Me too!'

CHAPTER
Nine

Lauren didn't sleep very well that night. She couldn't stop worrying about Currant. It was so strange that he hadn't been able to fly. Why hadn't his magic been working?

I hope there's nothing wrong with him, she thought anxiously.

She was still wondering about him, when Mel rang after breakfast.

'Shall we go to Orchard Stables today?' she asked. 'Jess is busy but I could come and we could ride over to see Grace and then return through the woods and jump some logs.'

'OK,' Lauren agreed. She loved jumping over logs in the woods. 'Let's meet in half an hour.'

By the time Mel arrived, Lauren had tacked up Twilight. As they rode down the path they passed Max, Stephen and Leo.

Max and Stephen were doing some jumps over a rail and Leo, whose ankle was bandaged, was videoing them with Mr Foster's new camera.

'Make sure you get this jump, Leo!' Max begged.

'Then film me,' Stephen shouted.

'Hi!' Lauren called. 'What are you guys doing?'

Stephen and Max skateboarded over.

'We're making a skateboarding video,' Stephen told her.

'Leo's brilliant at filming!' Max added.

Leo grinned. 'The doctor said I can't skateboard for two weeks, so Stephen suggested we make a video to send to *Skateboarder* magazine. They're having a video competition.'

'Dad said that Leo can borrow the camera so long as Leo gives him some lessons on how to use it afterwards,' Max said.

'I'd rather be skateboarding,' Leo said.

'But filming skateboarding is almost as much fun. Come on, you guys,' he said to Max and Stephen, 'I want to film some more.'

Lauren felt a rush of happiness. Hopefully, when Leo started skateboarding again, he wouldn't feel like he had to do any more dangerous tricks to try and impress Stephen.

She clicked her tongue and Twilight walked on beside Shadow.

'I think it might rain,' Mel said, looking at the heavy grey sky overhead. 'We'd better trot.'

Lauren and Mel reached Orchard Stables just as the rain started to fall. Lauren was

glad she was wearing her long waterproof
riding coat.

'Bring Shadow and Twilight into the
barn,' Grace said, meeting them in
the yard. 'There's a stable free. They can
go in there if they don't mind sharing.'

Lauren and Mel put Shadow and
Twilight into the empty stable and
joined Grace at the barn entrance.
'I can't believe it's raining again,' she
sighed. 'I'd better bring the ponies in.'

'Do you want a hand?' Lauren offered.

'Thanks,' said Grace.

The three of them started to walk
down the path. 'Is Jo-Ann here today?'
Mel asked.

'No, she's at a show for three days,'

Grace said. 'She rang last night. Beauty won her class yesterday so Jo was really pleased.'

They talked about the show all the way to the field. The rain was heavier now and the ponies were standing by the gate.

'I'll bring Currant and Windfall,' Grace said, handing leadropes to Lauren and Mel. 'Can you bring the other four between you?'

The ponies were keen to come inside and it only took a few minutes to get them out of the field.

'Currant seems very quiet,' Mel commented. 'Doesn't he like the rain?'

Lauren looked at the foal. His head was low and he seemed very subdued.

'It's not just the rain,' Grace said. 'He's been like this all morning. He didn't even eat his breakfast.' She and Lauren exchanged quick glances.

When they reached the barn, Lauren hung back with Grace while Mel led Ziggy and Lemonade to their stalls.

'Do you think Currant's still upset about not being able to fly?' she whispered.

Grace nodded. 'I'm sure that's what's

bothering him. He was really quiet when I turned him back into a pony.'

'Poor Currant,' Lauren said. It was horrid seeing him look so sad. 'Let's meet again tonight and cheer him up.'

'OK,' Grace agreed. 'Same place and time?'

Lauren nodded and they led the ponies into the barn.

It rained off and on all day. By the time Lauren and Twilight flew to the woods that night, the rain had turned to drizzle. Looking down at the creek, Lauren noticed how full it was. The water was racing along much faster today. Twigs and leaves were being swept away in the strong current and swirls of water splashed over the island. Grace and Currant were standing in the middle of the island, where it was still dry.

'Hi!' Lauren called as Twilight landed beside Currant.

Grace said hello but Currant didn't say anything.

Twilight gave Currant a friendly push with his nose. 'Are we going to try flying again tonight?'

'I don't want to,' muttered Currant.

'Go on,' Grace encouraged him.

'You won't get better if you don't practise,' Twilight warned him.

'But what if I can't fly like last night?' Currant said.

'I bet you'll be fine,' Lauren told him. 'Just have a try.'

Currant trotted forward reluctantly and tried to canter upward, but his hooves didn't leave the ground. 'I can't do it!' he said, looking at them desperately.

'You *must* be able to,' Twilight said.

'I can't,' Currant said miserably.

'But all unicorns can fly,' Lauren protested.

Currant hung his head. 'All unicorns except me.'

'Oh, Currant . . .' Grace sighed. She reached out to hug him but he stepped away from her.

'I'm useless! I'm not a proper unicorn.

I'm too little and I can't do anything. I know you wish you had another unicorn instead of me!'

'Of course I don't wish that!' Grace exclaimed. 'I —'

She was interrupted by a low thundering noise. It seemed to come from further up in the mountains.

'What was that?' Twilight said.

'I don't know,' Lauren replied.

Grace looked alarmed. 'It sounded like a surge of water up in the mountains. It must be from all the rain.'

'I think you're right!' Lauren gasped as a wave of water rushed down the creek towards them. It swept over the bridge, submerging it completely. The water around the edge of the island started to rise until it had nearly reached the girls and their unicorns.

'How are we going to get back?' Grace exclaimed in alarm. 'The bridge is underwater!'

Lauren looked round but there was no other way off the island. Grace and Currant were trapped.

'Don't worry,' said Twilight. 'I'll fly Grace across.'

Lauren frowned. 'It could be dangerous! Don't you remember what happened when you tried to fly with Grace two days ago?'

Twilight scraped the ground with a hoof. 'Now Grace needs our help! I'm sure the unicorn magic will let her ride me.'

'What about Currant?' Grace cried.

Twilight looked very solemn. 'He'll *have* to fly.'

'But I can't!' Currant said in alarm.

'You can, Currant. All unicorns can fly,' Twilight insisted.

A fresh surge of water washed towards them, splashing Twilight's hooves.

Grace threw her arms round Currant's neck. 'You have to try,' she begged. 'You can't stay here. The island's going to be flooded!'

Currant stamped his front hooves, making the water splash. 'No! I can't do it! I can't!' he cried.

CHAPTER
Ten

A wave of water covered the last patch of grass. The island was completely flooded now.

'We've got to go!' Lauren shouted, swinging herself on to Twilight's back. 'Come on, Grace!' She grabbed Grace's hand and pulled her up too.

'Fly with us, Currant!' Grace pleaded.

Currant didn't move.

'Please!' Grace cried.

Currant looked terrified. 'But I'll fall into the water!'

Lauren leaned forward and spoke urgently to Twilight. 'Can't you use your horn to make Currant brave, like when you helped Shadow to jump?'

Being able to give people and ponies courage by touching them with his horn was one of Twilight's magic powers.

'It won't work,' Twilight replied. 'Currant already has a unicorn's courage. He just has to find it.' The floodwater had nearly reached his knees now. 'I'm going to have to take off!'

'Currant! Come on!' Lauren and Grace yelled as Twilight leapt into the sky.

Currant whinnied and reared up in fear.

'Currant!' Grace sobbed.

The little unicorn tried to canter after them, but he couldn't lift himself off the ground. His hooves struck helplessly at the air before splashing down into the water.

'Stop, Twilight!' Grace begged, tears running down her face. 'I can't leave Currant there! I just can't!'

Twilight swung round.

'I'm coming back, Currant!' Grace yelled.

Twilight swooped back to the island. The waves were lapping almost up to Currant's tummy. Twilight landed with a splash.

Grace scrambled off his back. 'Oh, Currant,' she said, flinging her arms round his neck. 'Keep trying!'

'I can't do it,' he said, his eyes wide with fear.

'You can!' Grace told him. She pulled back. 'I *know* you can do it, Currant.'

He stared at her. 'You really believe I can fly?'

Grace touched his forelock. 'Yes.

You're my magic unicorn. You can do anything.'

Currant looked into her eyes for a long moment.

'Please try again,' Grace whispered. 'For me.'

Suddenly Currant lifted his head. 'All right.'

'Hurry!' Grace cried as the creek's current nearly knocked her off her feet.

She raced back to Twilight and scrambled on behind Lauren.

Twilight galloped through the water. 'Follow me, Currant!'

Currant raced after him. Lauren twisted around to watch the little unicorn. His eyes shone, and at last

he looked as if he really believed he
could fly.

As Twilight took off, Currant plunged
into the air beside him and they
cantered upward together.

'You're flying, Currant!' Grace
exclaimed. 'You're really flying!'

Currant surged effortlessly through the
sky. Side by side, he and Twilight flew
over the swollen creek to the safety of
the woods on the other side.

Twilight swooped down through the
trees and landed on dry ground.

'Wow! Flying's amazing!' Grace gasped.

'I know,' Lauren grinned.

'Look at me!' cried Currant as he
circled above them. 'I'm doing it!' He

dived steeply before cantering up to the treetops and stopping to rear proudly in the air.

Lauren and Grace hugged each other in delight and Twilight whinnied happily.

'Here I come!' called Currant. He raced downward, pulling up as he got near to the ground. With a neat flick of his heels he landed beside Grace.

'That was brilliant!' Grace said.

Currant tossed his head. 'It was great!'

Grace hugged him. 'Oh, Currant, I'm so glad you managed to fly. I don't know what we'd have done if you hadn't. What made you able to do it?'

Currant nuzzled her. 'It was you, Grace. When you told me I was your unicorn and that you knew I could fly, I suddenly felt all different inside.'

Twilight snorted. 'It's because you're his Unicorn Friend, Grace,' he explained. 'You and Currant make his unicorn magic together.'

'What do you mean?' Grace asked curiously.

Lauren thought she understood what Twilight meant. 'I get it!' she exclaimed. 'Currant needed to believe that you thought he could do it, Grace. Just like when we say the Turning Spell, we have to believe in it to make it happen. Well, a unicorn needs to think their Unicorn Friend believes in him or his magic won't work. Currant couldn't fly because

he didn't think you believed he could
and so his magic stopped working!'

Twilight nodded. 'You're right, Lauren.
Currant stopped being able to fly when
Grace said he was too little and
shouldn't keep trying.'

Currant looked up at Grace with
wide eyes.

'Oh, Currant,' Grace said in dismay. 'I
just wanted you to stop for a bit. I
didn't want you to hurt yourself. I never
once thought that you *couldn't* fly.'

Currant hung his head. 'I thought you
did. I thought you were wishing you
had a different unicorn, a proper
unicorn like Twilight, who was really
good at magic.'

'But you're the best unicorn ever!' Grace exclaimed, hugging him. 'I'd never want a different unicorn!'

'Really?' Currant asked anxiously.

Grace nodded her head. 'Really.'

'Even though you won't be able to go flying with me for a couple of years?'

'That doesn't matter,' Grace told him. 'Flying on Twilight was great, but having you as my unicorn is much more important. There'll be plenty of time for us to go flying when you're older. We've still got to learn all about your magic powers and how to make them work – together.'

Currant nuzzled her hair. 'Yes, together.'

Lauren put her hand on Twilight's mane. He blew softly on her cheek. 'Should we go home?' he suggested.

Lauren nodded. She had a feeling that Grace and Currant wanted to be on their own for a while before they headed back to the stables.

As Lauren got on to Twilight's back,
Grace glanced round. 'Thanks for rescuing
me, Twilight.' She smiled at him. 'You're
the second best unicorn in the whole
world!' she said, her smile widening.

Twilight snorted and Currant looked
delighted. He stamped a hoof. 'Next
time we meet up, Twilight, we can have
a flying race.' He gave a cheeky toss of
his head. 'Bet I'll beat you!'

'I'd like to see you try!' Twilight
teased the foal as he swept into the sky
with Lauren on his back.

'Bye!' they both called.

But Grace and Currant didn't hear
them. They were too busy talking, their
heads so close they were touching.

Lauren smiled. That was how it should be — a secret unicorn alone with his special Unicorn Friend. 'I'm glad Grace and Currant are happy now,' she said. 'I can't believe Currant actually thought Grace wanted a different unicorn.'

'I know. You'd never want another unicorn but me, would you?' Twilight said.

'Well, actually . . .' Lauren teased.

Twilight gave a little buck.

'Of course I'd never want another unicorn,' Lauren reassured him. 'You're perfect.' She leant forward and hugged him tightly. 'Whatever Grace says, you're the best unicorn in the world, Twilight,' she said. 'The *very* best.'

'And you're the best Unicorn Friend,

Lauren!' Twilight said with a whinny of
delight.

He galloped faster over the trees.
Lauren's hair flew out behind her, and
together they swooped upward, chasing
the stars.

My Secret Unicorn

When Lauren recites a secret spell, her pony Twilight
turns into a beautiful unicorn with magical powers!
Together Lauren and Twilight learn how to
use their magic to help their friends.

The Magic Spell
Linda Chapman

Dreams Come True
Linda Chapman

Flying High
Linda Chapman

Starlight Surprise
Linda Chapman

Stronger Than Magic
Linda Chapman

A Special Friend
Linda Chapman

A Touch of Magic
Linda Chapman

Twilight Magic
Linda Chapman

Friends Forever
Linda Chapman

Rising Star
Linda Chapman

Look out for more *My Secret Unicorn* adventures

Cover illustrations © Andrew Farley